T0198418

Inspiration From the Garden of Flora

JANET HILL

WestBow Press books may be ordered through booksellers or by contacting:

WestBow Press
A Division of Thomas Nelson & Zondervan
1663 Liberty Drive
Bloomington, IN 47403
www.westbowpress.com
844-714-3454

Interior Image Credit: Janet Hill

ISBN: 978-1-6642-7668-0 (sc)
ISBN: 978-1-6642-7669-7 (e)

Library of Congress Control Number: 2022916091

Print information available on the last page.

WestBow Press rev. date: 09/09/2022

WESTBOW
P R E S S®
A DIVISION OF THOMAS NELSON
& ZONDERVAN

Dedication

This collection of "Flora Inspires" is lovingly dedicated to my family. Family means everything to me. The love and encouragement shown to me by my husband of 43 years and our 2 adult kids had kept me going and helped make Flora a reality. My late mother was the biggest inspiration of my life. She was creative, artistic, loving, and the most positive person you could ever meet. She always had a big hug, a sweet smile, and so many positives to offer. In essence, Flora WAS my mom!

Goals

Education

It's worth every step!

– Flora

Share what
you have.

– Flora

Just for you
from Flora

Share your heart

– Flora

If you see someone who
doesn't have a smile...
give them one of yours

– Flora

6

Don't bottle up
your feelings

– Flora

Sometimes, all you need is a different perspective.

– Flora

You're my pick!

— Flora

Leave your troubles at the door.

-Flora

Daisies make days brighter!

– Flora

Keep your chin up!

– Flora

ICE CREAM
5¢

There's a rainbow
somewhere.

– Flora

Napping isn't
just for cats!

– Flora

Show them your
true colors.

– Flora

Dance in the rain.

– Flora

Close your eyes and just listen.

– Flora

Try something new.
– Flora

It's ok to get dirty!

– Flora

1, 2, 3, 4, 5, 6, 7, 8, 9, 10.... Count your blessings.

— Flora

Make a wish

– Flora

Unplug and unwind.

– Flora

You reap what you sow.

– Flora

Make a wish

– Flora

Let's look at the world
through rose colored glasses!

– Flora

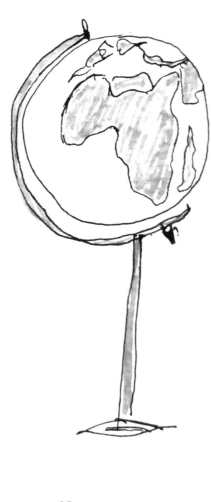

Start your day on
a happy note.

– Flora

You can't fix
everything
– Flora

Write your own story.

– Flora

Express yourself

– Flora

When you can't hear the music,
dance to your heartbeat!

−Flora

A worm and a fishing pole is just the beginning of a relaxing afternoon!

– Flora

Printed in the United States
by Baker & Taylor Publisher Services